Magic Bunny

Vacation Dreams

SUE BENTLEY

illustrated by Angela Swan

Grosset & Dunlap
An Imprint of Penguin Group (USA) Inc.

Please help the bunnies of Moonglow Meadow!

Our brave and loyal friend, Arrow, has traveled far from our world to protect the magic key that keeps our kingdom safe from the dark rabbits. Arrow is very far from home and will need your help.

Could you be his friend?

This magic bunny might be hard to spot as he is very small and often appears in different fluffy bunny disguises—but you can recognize him by the rainbow twinkle in his eyes.

Thank you for your help!

Strike
Leader of Moonglow Meadow

To Daisy, cute and fluffy, lop-eared
childhood friend—SB

GROSSET & DUNLAP
Published by the Penguin Group
Penguin Group (USA) Inc., 375 Hudson Street,
New York, New York 10014, USA
Penguin Group (Canada), 90 Eglinton Avenue East,
Suite 700, Toronto, Ontario M4P 2Y3, Canada
(a division of Pearson Penguin Canada Inc.)
Penguin Books Ltd, 80 Strand, London WC2R 0RL, England
Penguin Ireland, 25 St. Stephen's Green, Dublin 2, Ireland
(a division of Penguin Books Ltd)
Penguin Group (Australia), 707 Collins Street, Melbourne, Victoria 3008, Australia
(a division of Pearson Australia Group Pty Ltd)
Penguin Books India Pvt Ltd, 11 Community Center,
Panchsheel Park, New Delhi—110 017, India
Penguin Group (NZ), 67 Apollo Drive, Rosedale, Auckland 0632, New Zealand
(a division of Pearson New Zealand Ltd)
Penguin Books, Rosebank Office Park, 181 Jan Smuts Avenue,
Parktown North 2193, South Africa
Penguin China, B7 Jaiming Center, 27 East Third Ring Road North,
Chaoyang District, Beijing 100020, China

Penguin Books Ltd, Registered Offices:
80 Strand, London WC2R 0RL, England

Text copyright © 2010 Sue Bentley. Illustrations copyright © 2010 Angela Swan.
Cover illustration © 2010 Andrew Farley. First printed as *Holiday Dreams* in
Great Britain in 2010 by Puffin Books. First published in the United States in 2013
by Grosset & Dunlap, a division of Penguin Young Readers Group,
345 Hudson Street, New York, New York 10014. GROSSET & DUNLAP
is a trademark of Penguin Group (USA) Inc. Printed in the U.S.A.

Library of Congress Cataloging-in-Publication Data is available.

ISBN 978-0-448-46728-3   10 9 8 7 6 5 4 3 2

Prologue

Arrow looked around at Moonglow Meadow. Many of his fellow magic rabbits were hopping around on the dry patchy ground while others were nibbling wilted plants. He had returned just in time.

The tiny gold key he wore on a chain around his neck glowed brightly and a cloud of crystal dust rose into the air. It sprinkled down gently and a lush carpet of fresh grass and brightly colored wildflowers appeared and spread until it covered the whole meadow.

The hungry rabbits began to eat. Some of the younger ones rolled over and over, getting the scent of the dewy grass on their fur.

An older rabbit hopped toward Arrow. He had a dark gray muzzle and wore a wise expression.

"Strike!" Arrow bowed his head in greeting before the leader of the warren.

"It is good to see you again, Arrow," Strike said in a deep velvety voice. "We chose well when we made you keeper of our magic key."

Arrow felt a surge of pride at the leader's praise. He knew that he would guard the key with his life.

Suddenly, there was a commotion at the far side of Moonglow Meadow and Arrow saw a group of rabbits rushing toward them.

"The-the dark rabbits are coming!" one of them squealed, wide-eyed with panic.

Arrow flattened his silver-tipped ears nervously. The dark rabbits lived nearby in a deep gully. The land had become so dry that nothing grew there and they were hungry, but the dark rabbits had refused Strike's invitation to live with them in Moonglow Meadow.

"They are coming to steal our magic key," Strike rumbled, "and use it to make their gully green and beautiful again."

"But without the key's power, Moonglow Meadow will become a desert!" Arrow gasped.

"That is why you must go to the Otherworld once more," Strike said gravely. "Hide there so the dark rabbits cannot find the key!"

Arrow felt very young and scared, but he knew the warren was relying on him. "I will do it!"

Strike gave a soft but piercing cry.

Every rabbit in the warren came speeding toward them and formed a circle around Arrow. Suddenly, the golden key hanging from Arrow's neck glowed very brightly.

The light slowly faded and where the pure white-and-silver magic rabbit had been now stood a tiny pale coffee-colored bunny with fluffy fur and huge brown eyes that twinkled with tiny rainbows.

"Go now! Use this disguise," Strike said. "Only return when Moonglow Meadow needs more of the key's magic. And watch out for the dark rabbits!"

Arrow held up his tiny fluffy head. "I will!"

Thud. Thud. Thud. The rabbits began thumping their feet in time. Arrow felt the magic building and a cloud of crystal dust shimmered around him as Moonglow Meadow grew fainter and fainter . . .

Chapter ONE

Becky Hodge woke early with a feeling of excitement. "Yay! It's vacation!" she cried, thinking of all the things she could do with her friends—tennis, swimming, maybe even horseback riding. She flung back the covers, almost falling out of bed in her eagerness to get up.

A shaft of early morning sunlight

streamed into the darkened room
through a heart-shaped hole in the
wooden shutters. Becky frowned in
puzzlement.

Wooden shutters? Her bedroom
didn't have . . .

And then she remembered where she
was. "Foxglove Farm!"

Becky was staying at her aunt and
uncle's farm while her mom and Aunty
Katy were away on a business trip.
They taught classes in country crafts and
knitting.

Even though it was a bit strange
being at the farm with only Uncle
Den and her cousin Leon, who played
computer games all day, at least there
was more to do on the farm than at her
house. Her dad was at home working

on an important assignment for his job and needed peace and quiet—and that was not how Becky wanted to spend her vacation!

"See if you can't drag Leon away from his computer for an hour or two," Dad had said as he kissed her good-bye last night. "If you can't, no one can!"

Becky grinned to herself as she

went to the bedroom shutters. Dad
was always teasing her about being too
enthusiastic and not taking no for an
answer.

She stood looking out at the view
of the farmyard with its huge barns and
fields full of corn and vegetables.

There was the faint outline of a
village far away in the distance; beyond
that, all she could see were thick woods
and the green slopes of rolling hills.

Becky sighed as she turned away
from the window. The farm was miles
from any other people. She had no
choice but to make the best of things.

As she dressed in jeans and a T-shirt,
she tried hard to think of something
Leon might like doing besides playing
computer games. Soccer! All boys liked

that, didn't they? Maybe she could persuade him to come outside and play.

She was pulling on her sneakers when there was a knock at the door.

"Come in!" Becky called.

Leon stuck his head around the door. He had sandy hair that flopped over his forehead and serious blue eyes. At twelve years old, he was three years older than Becky.

"Hi, Leon! Do you want to kick the soccer ball around later? I'm pretty good at sports. Look!" Becky shuffled her feet encouragingly as if she was dribbling a ball. But in her eagerness she caught the toe of her sneaker on the rug and almost tripped.

Leon looked at her curiously. "Er, sorry, I can't. I've got stuff to finish."

"Oh . . . okay. Well, when you're done, maybe we can do something together?" Becky tried again. "How about tennis or baseball? Or you could show me around those woods—"

"Maybe later." Leon edged out

of the doorway and called from the landing. "I only came to tell you that breakfast's ready!"

Becky tried to ignore a growing feeling of dismay as she followed her cousin downstairs. Maybe Leon didn't like hanging around with younger kids. Whenever Becky was here, he always stayed in his room.

Uncle Den sat at the kitchen table drinking tea and reading a farming magazine. He looked up and smiled as Becky came in. "Hello, honey. Did you sleep well?"

"Yes, thanks." Becky returned his smile and sat down next to Leon, who was staring into space as if he was deep in thought.

"This is Mrs. Kelly." Her uncle

nodded toward a small round figure bustling about at the stove. He explained that she'd be doing the cooking and house-keeping while Becky's aunt was away.

"Hello, Mrs. Kelly," Becky said cheerfully.

"Good morning." Mrs. Kelly smiled back at Becky, but only briefly. Her gray hair was pinned into a neat bun and a spotless apron covered her blue flowered dress. She placed a steaming dish of eggs, bacon, and sausage on the table, followed by a stack of toast.

"Here you go. Help yourselves."

Becky could feel her tummy rumbling at the sight of the feast in front of her. She began loading her plate.

While they all ate, the housekeeper

washed pots and pans at the speed of light. She then strode into the laundry room next to the kitchen. Becky heard a whooshing sound as the washing machine went into action.

"I'll be giving those bed sheets a good airing," Mrs. Kelly said loudly, to no one in particular. "I don't use those new-fangled tumble-dryers."

What's the big deal? Becky wondered. *Mom dries our laundry—doesn't everyone?*

Becky finished everything on her plate. She was just enjoying some toast with butter and jam when Leon stood up and asked to be excused from the table. "It's okay, isn't it, Dad? I've got something really important to do."

"Sure, go ahead. But I don't want you shut away upstairs for hours on

end while Becky's staying with us,"
his father said. "I'm relying on you to
entertain our guest."

"Yeah, of course I will. I just have
to finish this first!" Leon said over his
shoulder, already rushing out.

Becky heard him clattering upstairs
and then slamming his bedroom door.

Uncle Den shook his head slowly
as he turned to Becky. "Leon writes
a column for an online magazine—or
''zine' as he calls it. He takes it very
seriously. Do you like computers,
honey?"

"They're okay. But I get bored
sitting down all the time," Becky
replied. "I usually prefer being outside
and doing stuff."

"An action girl, eh? Sounds like

you'll be good for Leon!"

Becky smiled, hoping he was right.
But things didn't look too promising.
Leon hadn't shown much interest in
spending any time with her so far.

Uncle Den began reading the
classifieds. A kitchen clock ticked loudly
in the silence.

Becky finished her toast. She leaned

forward and propped her cheek on one hand, wondering what she might do next. *Is it worth going upstairs and trying to persuade Leon to come exploring with me or should I just go on my own?*

"There will be no elbows on the table, young lady, if you don't mind!" A stern voice spoke close to her ear as Mrs. Kelly reached for Becky's empty plate.

Becky almost jumped out of her skin. "Um . . . sorry."

She blushed as she quickly leaned back and put her hands in her lap. No one minded about stuff like that at home.

Uncle Den put down his magazine and stood up. "Don't worry about Mrs. Kelly. She has very high standards. But

her bark's a lot worse than her bite,"
he said, winking at her. "Well—I have
a rabbit problem to look into. The little
devils have been playing havoc with
my crops and I have got to take some
serious action. You and Leon have a
good day. If you need anything, just ask
Mrs. Kelly."

"Okay. See you later," Becky said.

Mrs. Kelly was now sliding a floor
mop under the table. As it almost
whisked across her sneakers, Becky
leaped up out of her chair and headed
into the back garden. The housekeeper
was seriously scary.

It had been raining earlier, but the
sun was shining now and everything
smelled fresh. Becky made her way
around the side of the house. One of

the farm workers was driving a tractor across the farmyard and another was coming out of the barn. They smiled and waved at her so Becky waved back.

She spotted a gate that led into a field with a duck pond. She went through and wandered over the damp grass.

There were a number of wild rabbits

hopping about in the next field, their white cottontails flashing.

"Watch out! Uncle Den will be after you if you get into his crops!" she warned them.

Suddenly, there was a bright flash and a shower of crystal dust drifted toward her in a twinkling cloud.

"Oh!" Becky narrowed her eyes, trying to peer through it. As the dust slowly cleared, she spotted a fluffy pale coffee-colored bunny on the grass right in front of her.

"Can you help me, please?" it asked in a scared little voice.

Chapter TWO

Becky's jaw dropped and she stared at the cute little bunny in total amazement. Perhaps it was someone's pet. She didn't know a lot about pet bunnies, but she was pretty sure that they couldn't talk.

She laughed at herself. Just because Leon wouldn't talk to her, it didn't mean a rabbit would!

The pale brown bunny's little pink

nose twitched nervously and it looked
up at her with huge eyes like chocolate
drops.

Becky edged closer and slowly bent
down, trying not to frighten it.

"Hello. Aren't you sweet?" she
crooned. "You don't seem all that scared
of me. Do you want to be friends?"

"Yes. I would like that very much,"

the bunny said in a trembly little voice.

"Whoa!" Becky gasped in shock. She lost her balance and sat down hard on the damp grass. "You . . . you really can talk!"

"Yes. All of my warren can talk. I am Arrow, guardian of Moonglow Meadow," the cute bunny told her, his long floppy ears lifting proudly. "What is your name?"

"Um . . . Rebecca. Rebecca Hodge. But everyone calls me Becky. This is my uncle's farm. I'm staying here while my mom and aunt are away on business." She noticed that Arrow's deep-brown eyes seemed to be glimmering with tiny rainbows.

The bunny bowed his head. "I am honored to meet you, Becky."

"Me too." Becky moved onto her knees, wondering if she should curtsy or something, but she finally settled for just dipping her chin. "Is Moonglow Meadow another one of Uncle Den's fields?"

"No. It is far from here. In another world," Arrow explained. As he lifted his chin, something around his neck twinkled. Becky saw that he wore a fine gold chain with a key hanging from it.

"What's that?" she asked him.

"The magic key, which I must keep safe from the fierce dark rabbits. Their land is dry and stony and they are hungry, but they refuse to share our land with us. They want to steal the key and use it to make only their land lush and green. But if they do this, Moonglow Meadow will become a desert."

"Oh no! That would be terrible!" Becky exclaimed.

"Yes. I will not let it happen!" A determined look crossed Arrow's fluffy face. "That is why I agreed to come here all by myself."

Becky was still having trouble taking all this in, but fascination was starting to take over from shock. Arrow's world sounded so strange and magical.

She smiled warmly at him. "You're very brave for such a tiny bunny."

Arrow raised himself onto his back legs and flicked his tail mischievously.

"I am not so small. Please stay back!" he ordered.

Becky felt a weird warm tingling

sensation down her spine as the key around Arrow's neck began flashing and a cloud of twinkling crystal dust swirled around him. When it cleared Becky saw that the little bunny had disappeared and in his place was the most stunning rabbit she had ever seen. It was as big as a large cat and had silky white fur, flecked with silver. The tips of its ears twinkled with what looked like molten silver, and big jewel-bright rainbows flashed from its eyes.

Becky gasped in amazement. She'd never seen anything so majestic or so beautiful.

"Arrow?" she gulped.

"Yes, Becky. It is still me," Arrow said in a smooth voice.

Before she had gotten used to seeing

him in his true form, there was a final
flash of light from his key and Arrow
reappeared as a pale coffee-colored
bunny.

"Wow! That's a cool disguise!"
Becky exclaimed.

Arrow twitched his nose nervously.
"I am afraid the dark rabbits will see
through it if they catch up with me. I
must find a place to hide, and quickly."

Becky's heart went out to the brave little bunny. She wanted to do all she could to help him. "You can live in my bedroom. Wait until I tell my cousin Leon about you. He might even talk to me then and—"

"No, I am sorry, Becky, my mission is secret. You can tell no one. Please promise me," the magic bunny asked anxiously.

Becky felt a little bit disappointed. She had been hoping that Leon would want to spend more time with her if he saw that she had a magical new friend. But she also felt proud that Arrow was prepared to trust her with such an important secret.

"Okay, then, I promise," she agreed. "I'll smuggle you into the farmhouse.

No one's going to notice. Mrs. Kelly will be too busy doing housework and Leon's on his computer. He doesn't even seem that interested in me being here."

Arrow dipped his head gratefully. "I would like to stay with you very much. Thank you, Becky."

"You're welcome!" Becky scooted toward him on her knees and reached

out her cupped hands. Arrow jumped straight into them.

She felt him snuggle up against her as she stood up. A happy feeling glowed inside Becky as she thought about having a secret friend all to herself for this week—especially such an amazing one as Arrow!

Chapter
THREE

Becky cradled Arrow close as she walked back across the field. At the gate that opened onto the farmyard, she paused.

"We'll sneak in through the back door. I don't really want to bump into Mrs. Kelly," she said to Arrow. "Uh-oh!" she whispered, quickly ducking behind the gate as the farmhouse door opened and the house-keeper appeared.

Becky didn't want to have to answer awkward questions if she was caught with Arrow, so she crouched out of sight until Mrs. Kelly went off toward the henhouse.

"Phew! That was close!" Becky slipped through the gate and, cuddling Arrow close, sprinted across the yard and slipped around to the back of the farmhouse.

She looked down at her new friend as she walked across the lawn. Arrow was so cute. He had stretched up to lie full-length against her chest, and his eyes were closed contentedly as she stroked his pale fur. It was the softest thing she had ever touched.

"Oh!" Becky felt something very big and wet flap against her face.

A bed sheet! She hadn't been looking where she was going and had stumbled into a line of clean laundry. A gust of wind made a corner of the sheet flick over Becky's shoulder with a cracking sound.

Arrow gave a squeal of terror and tried to leap out of her arms.

"It's okay, Arrow, it's only a sheet!"

But the terrified magic bunny didn't seem to be listening. He kicked out with his back legs, accidentally scratching Becky's chest through her T-shirt.

Becky winced at the stinging soreness, but she made herself ignore it as she struggled to keep hold of her tiny friend without squeezing him too hard. She was worried that he'd hurt himself if he jumped to the ground from such a height. But her sneakers slipped on the damp grass and Becky felt herself tumbling forward. Stretching out one hand, she grabbed at the nearest sheet to save herself.

Snap! Snap! Snap! Clothes pegs pinged off the line as Becky collapsed into a heap of wet washing.

"Ooof!" She managed to twist

around and land on her back, keeping
Arrow safe in her cupped hands. Becky
lay there for a moment, too stunned
to move. She could feel Arrow's rapid
heartbeat against her palm.

"Are you okay?" Becky asked him
worriedly.

"I am fine. You saved me. Thank
you!" Arrow moved up to nudge her
chin gently with his little wet nose.

Relief washed through Becky. She'd
only had Arrow for a short time, but
she already loved her magical friend to
pieces and couldn't bear to think of him
being hurt.

She struggled to get free of the
clinging damp material.

"Oh!" As Becky finally managed to
stand up, the stinging came back. Now

that the excitement was over, the claw
marks Arrow had made in his panic
were starting to hurt horribly.

Arrow laid his ears flat with concern.
"You are hurt, Becky. Let me help
you!"

Becky saw Arrow's key start to pulse
with light and felt a warm tingling
sensation down her spine. He twitched
his little pink nose and a fountain of
crystal dust appeared, shimmering with a
thousand tiny rainbows.

To Becky's amazement, the magical
dust spread all over the front of her
T-shirt, before seeming to sink into
it and disappear. The scratch marks
turned cold and then stopped hurting
completely as if they'd never been there
at all.

When Becky peered down inside her
T-shirt to check, there wasn't a single
mark to be seen.

"Cool! Thanks, Arrow. I'm fine now.
Come on. Let's get you inside before—"

"My laundry!" boomed a furious
voice. "What have you done, you silly
girl?"

Becky froze in terror. She slowly
turned to see Mrs. Kelly standing in the

kitchen doorway. She was staring at Becky's feet.

Becky looked down, too, horrified to see that she was standing on a heap of trampled muddy sheets. She had been so worried about Arrow that she hadn't given a thought to the laundry.

"I am in so much trouble!" Becky groaned, expecting a double scolding. She was still holding the fluffy bunny, who was now tucked safely under one arm. Mrs. Kelly seemed the sort who wouldn't allow animals into the house.

"Just look at those sheets!" The housekeeper marched into the garden with a face like thunder. Becky leaped backward in alarm, leaving another perfect muddy footprint on a clean bit of sheet.

"It was an . . . um . . . accident," she burbled lamely. "Sorry."

"A likely story!" Mrs. Kelly looked as if steam might come out of her ears at any moment. "Help me pick up these sheets and bring them into the house. It will all have to be done again. I have to go down the lane to Buttercup Farm, so since you're the one who made them all muddy, *you're* going to be the one to wash them!"

For some reason, Mrs. Kelly hadn't mentioned Arrow. It was almost as if she couldn't see him.

"Me! Do laundry? But I've never—" Becky began and then stopped as Mrs. Kelly gave her a stern look. "Fine. Will you show me how the washing machine works?"

"That's better. Follow me."

The moment the housekeeper's back
was turned, Becky quickly hid Arrow
under her T-shirt. She sighed. This was
terrible. The last thing she'd expected
to be doing on the first day of her farm
vacation was washing sheets!

Chapter
FOUR

Becky sat cross-legged on the laundry room floor, where she'd been for the past ten minutes, staring glumly at the washing machine. Mrs. Kelly had gone out after giving Becky strict orders not to move a muscle until all the sheets were done.

"That woman is superscary. I bet she'll tell on me to Uncle Den and insist that he grounds me! And how come she didn't seem to notice I was holding you?" she asked Arrow, who sat in her lap, calmly grooming himself.

The magic bunny looked up at Becky, the tip of his little pink tongue still sticking out.

"I used my magic, so that only you can see and hear me."

"You can make yourself invisible? Cool!" Becky smiled, wondering what else her magical friend could do. "I wish that could help us do the washing. These sheets are taking a long time. We might be here for a while."

Arrow put his head on one side. "I do not think so."

Becky felt the familiar tingling sensation down her back as Arrow's magic key began pulsing again with a glowing light. Another cloud of sparkling crystal dust appeared and trickled down onto the washing machine. The machine started whizzing around at superfast speed. Becky's eyes widened in amazement as it stopped dead with a

loud burping noise. The door flew open and out came the clean sheets, floating through the air like ghosts and drifting out of the back door.

Becky scrambled to her feet and ran after them. She was just in time to see the sheets drape themselves magically over the washing line.

Snap! Snap! Snap! A row of unused clothes pegs, dangling from the line, marched toward the sheets like a line of soldiers and clipped themselves smartly into place.

Becky clapped her hands in delight. "That was amazing! Thanks, Arrow. That would have been a horrible job. Let's go upstairs now and I can show you my bedroom."

Becky and Arrow had just reached the landing when Leon's bedroom door opened.

"What was all that shouting downstairs earlier?" he asked curiously.

Becky stiffened and started to hide Arrow behind her back before she remembered that he was invisible.

"That was Mrs. Kelly. She blew up at me!" she told him, rolling her eyes.

"Why?" Leon asked.

Becky told him about tripping over the sheets, being careful not to mention anything about Arrow. She was halfway through explaining when Leon began grinning and then laughing out loud.

"I wish I'd seen her face when she saw you trampling her clean laundry! You're a lot braver than I am!"

Becky looked at him in astonishment.
Someone seemed to have stolen her
quiet, serious cousin and put this boy
with the infectious laugh in his place.
She found herself smiling with him and
then both of them fell over laughing.

"Killer Kelly was so angry! I thought
her apron was going to come right
off, like the clothes pegs!" she gasped,

dabbing at her eyes with her T-shirt.

"Killer Kelly? That really suits her!" Leon laughed, holding his ribs.

Arrow watched them both from Becky's arms, with a look of puzzlement in his big soft brown eyes. He shook his head slowly.

"Humans are very strange sometimes."

Becky laughed even more. "Arr— um . . . I mean . . . *anyway*," she quickly corrected herself. She would have to be a lot more careful about keeping Arrow a secret. "I washed the sheets in double-quick time. I was just going up to my room because I don't want to be around when Mrs. Kelly gets back."

"I don't blame you." Leon looked thoughtful. "Come on!" he said, edging past her and starting to walk downstairs.

"Where are we going?"

"Somewhere I often go. Somewhere secret," he said mysteriously.

Becky was intrigued by the fact that her cousin was including her in something for the first time ever. She didn't need telling twice. "You're on!"

Arrow nudged Becky gently, obviously as eager as she was about having an adventure. She tucked him more securely under her arm before hurrying after Leon. It wasn't a moment too soon. As Becky, Arrow, and Leon crossed the kitchen, they heard the front door opening.

"Hello, Becky," Mrs. Kelly called. "How's that laundry doing?"

"Run!" Becky whispered.

Leon shot out of the kitchen door and headed down to the garden. Becky raced after him, but slowed down when she saw the tall, prickly hawthorn hedge that formed a barrier at the bottom.

"It's a dead end!"

"No, it's not! This way!" Leon kneeled down and wriggled through a gap near the ground that Becky hadn't noticed.

She put Arrow down so he could hop through and then picked him up again after she emerged. "Are you okay?" she whispered.

"I am fine." He settled in her arms again.

Leon looked back at her and frowned. Becky realized he had heard her.

"Just talking to myself. It's a habit of mine!" she said, scrambling upright.

They jogged down a narrow strip of grass that ran along the edge of a cornfield. Leon was ahead of her and just turning onto a rough track.

Becky ran after him. This was fun—like doing cross-country at school!

After a couple of minutes, Leon paused. "That's where we're going," he said, pointing to a hill that rose above the farm.

Becky shaded her eyes to look at it. It was mainly grass with just a few scrubby bushes on the slopes.

"What's so special about it?" she whispered to Arrow, as Leon quickened his pace again. "Maybe there are really good views from the top or something."

Arrow nodded.

Tall heads of corn rustled in the warm breeze and skylarks called overhead as they jogged onward. Becky could see the woods she'd glimpsed from her bedroom window and the towering shapes of other hills much farther away.

She'd almost caught up with Leon now. Picking up the pace, she caught up to him and then ran past him, her sneakers pounding the ground.

"Last one to the top loses!" she cried.

"No, wait!" Leon cried.

But Becky took no notice as she sped away. "Eat my dust!" she crowed.

Holding Arrow didn't slow her down. Even cradling him carefully, Becky was a fast runner. They reached the hilltop seconds ahead of Leon.

"Yay!" she cried triumphantly.

Panting, Leon pushed back a strand
of damp blond hair as he caught up
with her. "Are you always like this?"

"Pretty much!" Becky said, grinning.
She bent her knees to let Arrow jump
down and flopped onto the grass while
he hopped over to a patch of clover.

"I was *trying* to tell you that we have
to be quiet up here if we want to see
anything," Leon told her, sounding a bit
miffed. "The wild rabbits that live here
are used to me, but you're a stranger so
they might take longer to come out."

"Oh, sorry." Becky smiled sheepishly.
She did get carried away sometimes. She
turned over onto her tummy to watch
Arrow nibbling the juicy leaves. *Even if*

the wild rabbits are feeling shy, I can see one
special bunny right now!

Just then Arrow's ears twitched and
his big brown eyes glowed with tiny
rainbows as he looked more closely
at the hilltop. "There is a warren

here. Like back home in Moonglow Meadow!"

He gave a mighty leap, followed by three hops and disappeared down the nearest burrow.

Chapter
FIVE

"Arrow!" Becky gasped in shock, only just managing not to leap straight to her feet and take off after him.

Why had he run away? She hoped the magic bunny hadn't decided that he'd rather hide among his wild cousins.

"Why did you say "arrow"?" Leon asked, looking at Becky curiously.

"Oh, well . . . um . . ." Becky

didn't know quite how to answer without giving away the little magic bunny. But luckily, Leon forgot their conversation.

"Look!" He grabbed Becky's arm and pointed toward a large grayish-colored rabbit emerging from a burrow a couple of yards away. Its nose twitched as it stood up on its back legs, watchful and alert. "That's Smudge—at least that's

what I call her because of that brown mark on her right ear. She's the top female."

"Smudge?" Becky echoed, too worried about Arrow to concentrate properly.

She hesitated, trying to decide what to do. Her instincts told her to go closer to the warren and check out some of the burrows for any sign of her friend. But how could she explain that to Leon without giving Arrow away? She'd come really close already.

Becky forced herself to calm down. As hard as it was to wait, she would have to trust Arrow.

Leon was watching as other rabbits emerged. Soon, more adults stood up on their legs all around the warren, sniffing the air for possible enemies. Then, at some kind of invisible signal, six of the tiniest rabbits Becky had ever seen appeared from a burrow right beside Smudge.

"Look at those. Aren't they sweet?" Leon turned toward her to whisper. "Baby rabbits are called kits. This is the first time I've seen them out of their burrows. Smudge has been feeding them milk in a special underground chamber, until they're old enough to eat grass."

Becky's heart melted. They were very cute.

Suddenly, she spotted a familiar tiny fluffy pale coffee-colored shape hopping toward Smudge. Arrow!

"There he is!" Becky exclaimed. "I

mean . . . there they are," she quickly corrected herself, pointing at the kits.

Becky watched closely as Arrow stopped in front of Smudge. The tiny magic bunny looked about half the size of the lead female. Smudge laid her ears flat and her eyes rolled as she reared up above him with her front paws outstretched.

Smudge was going to attack Arrow!

Becky caught her breath, worried that her friend would be hurt. But the wild rabbit eventually sank back down and crouched head to head with Arrow. The two rabbits stayed motionless for a few seconds before Arrow touched his pink nose to the wild rabbit's muzzle. Smudge bowed her head as if in farewell.

To Becky's relief, she saw the magic bunny give a flick of his tail as he hopped away from the warren and came bounding back toward her. Becky felt her tension easing as the little rabbit settled down with his warm furry body pressed against her bare arm. Leon was busy looking at the kits, so Becky risked talking to Arrow.

"When you ran off like that, I thought you'd gone to live with the wild rabbits and didn't want to be my friend anymore," she whispered.

Arrow's floppy little ears drooped. "I am sorry. I should have explained that I was only exploring. I am very happy with you, Becky."

"That's okay, then." Becky stroked his fluffy fur, feeling a bit silly now for being so worried. "Because I love having you for my friend!"

They settled down together to watch the wild rabbits. Becky was able to concentrate properly now. She noticed quite a lot of difference in the colors of their fur. Some of the rabbits were a dark brown and others were almost gray.

Leon edged closer on his tummy and started scribbling in a notebook as he studied another group of larger rabbits that Becky assumed were males. She was really enjoying being here with him. Maybe being quiet sometimes wasn't so bad after all.

"The lead female is a nice rabbit," Arrow told her.

"Leon calls her Smudge," Becky whispered back. "Because of the mark on her ear."

Arrow nodded approval. "Smudge. That is a good name."

All at once, Becky noticed that the key around Arrow's neck was shining brightly.

Arrow saw her looking. "Moonglow Meadow will soon be in need of more of the key's magic," he explained.

"Do you have to leave?" Becky whispered anxiously.

Arrow looked up at her with serious eyes. "Not yet. But if the key glows constantly, I might have to leave suddenly, without saying good-bye."

"But you can come back here again afterward, can't you?"

Arrow shook his head. "I am afraid that is not possible, Becky. Once I leave here, the magic trail to this place is closed forever. I hope you understand," he said gently.

Becky pressed her lips together as she nodded, hoping that this wouldn't happen too soon. She had barely recovered from the fright Arrow had given her when he had wandered off, and she wanted to enjoy every single moment she could with him.

Sitting back in the warm sunshine, Becky, Arrow, and Leon watched the wild rabbits all around them. The creatures fed and groomed themselves, perfectly at ease.

Leon gave a muffled cry of delight as some of the kits leaped high in the air and kicked out with their tiny back legs so that they changed direction.

"Did you see that? Rabbits do that twisting jumping thing when they're happy. It's called a binky."

Becky felt her interest quickening.

She hadn't seen Arrow do a binky.
Maybe magic bunnies showed they were
happy in other ways. "How come you
know all this stuff?" she asked Leon.

"I've been reading up about wild
rabbits. Most people just take them for
granted, but they're really interesting
once you start looking more closely."

"I didn't realize that." Becky was
impressed. There was more to her

cousin than she'd realized. "Is this the kind of stuff you write about for the online 'zine Uncle Den told me about?"

"Yep. And tons of other stuff about animals and insects. I'm going to be a wildlife reporter when I'm older."

Becky believed him. "I think you'd be great at it."

Leon looked pleased but then he frowned. "I don't think I'll ever convince Dad about rabbits, though. He's always complaining that they're eating his crops and he's been threatening to do something about it."

"Yes. He mentioned that at breakfast, just after you went upstairs," Becky said.

"Did he?" Leon asked worriedly. "I wonder what he has in mind."

Becky searched her memory. "He

said he was going to 'take action' or something like that. Maybe he's going to trap them and then let them free somewhere else?"

"I wish," Leon said. A serious look flickered across his face. "There are lots of harsher ways to deal with a rabbit problem. If you ask me, this warren's in real danger."

Chapter SIX

It was late afternoon as Becky, Arrow, and Leon made their way back to the farmhouse. Leon was lagging behind, deep in thought. Becky knew he was worrying about the wild rabbits, as she was.

Arrow lay in the curve of Becky's arm, with his fluffy front paws crossed. "What did Leon mean about the warren being in danger?"

Becky wasn't exactly sure, but she had a fair idea. She hated telling him, but he would have to find out soon enough.

"Leon thinks Uncle Den is planning to use ways to . . . um . . . cut down the numbers of rabbits. Like getting rid of the warren," she said gently.

Arrow looked shocked. "That is terrible!"

Becky nodded, feeling awful. "Yes,
I know." She couldn't bear to think
of anything bad happening to the wild
rabbits, especially Smudge and her kits.

"There must be something we can
do!" Arrow said, his whiskers twitching
anxiously.

Becky racked her brain to come
up with a solution as they reached
the gap in the hawthorn hedge. She
had a sudden flare of hope when she
remembered how Arrow and Smudge
had stood head to head, as if they might
be communicating.

"Can magic bunnies talk to wild
rabbits?"

"No. We are only distantly related to
them. They do not speak our language.
But Smudge is a very intelligent rabbit.

I could sense some of her thoughts in pictures."

Becky hid her disappointment. "I thought you might be able to warn her about the danger, so she could tell the rabbits to stop eating the crops."

"I do not think that can happen. Did you notice how the plants around the hill have been nibbled down?" Arrow asked sadly. "The warren is large. I think there are too many hungry rabbits here."

Becky had a flash of inspiration. "I know! You could use the magic key to make the hill green and lush again—like Moonglow Meadow!"

Arrow nodded slowly. "It might work for a little while. But I will not always be here when the hill needs more magic. And the rabbits will be too hungry to resist eating your uncle's corn and cabbages again."

Becky realized she had to face facts. A solution didn't look very likely.

Dinner was a delicious lasagna and salad, made by Mrs. Kelly, who had already left to go home, much to Becky and Leon's relief.

Becky was sure the housekeeper must have told Uncle Den about the laundry incident. She waited expectantly for him to mention it, but nothing happened.

After dinner was cleared away, they all trooped into the sitting room. Leon wanted to watch a wildlife documentary about bats. Becky was looking forward

to it, too. She'd just curled up with
Arrow on her lap when her uncle
spoke. "Mrs. Kelly had a word with me
earlier . . ."

Becky held her breath. She steeled
herself for a serious scolding.

". . . about the chicken feed," her
uncle went on. "She noticed we were
getting low on supplies. Could you
order some more for me online, Leon?"

"Yep. No problem. I'll go and do it after this TV show."

Becky couldn't believe it. "Mrs. Kelly didn't tell on me!" she whispered to Arrow. "Maybe she isn't that bad after all."

Arrow was curling up into a furry ball. "I am glad you did not get into trouble," he said sleepily.

Becky smiled down at him. It had been a long day for a tiny bunny. "You have a nice nap," she whispered, gently cuddling him. She noticed Leon looking across at her and wondered if he'd noticed anything strange. Surely he couldn't see Arrow, who was still invisible?

But Leon gave Becky a shy smile. "You seemed to have a good time today. So I wondered if you'd like to see some of my wildlife stuff?"

"Yeah, I'd love to!" Becky said eagerly.

"Great! You can read the articles I've written for the 'zine, too, if you like."

"Don't push it!" Becky joked, rolling her eyes.

Leon laughed.

As she settled down to watch TV, Becky felt pleased that she and her cousin were getting along a bit better. She thought she'd definitely made the right decision to stay at the farmhouse. If only they could think of some way to help Smudge and the other rabbits, everything would be great.

The following day it rained. Becky
stared glumly out of the farmhouse
window at the deep puddles and muddy
ruts in the yard. She had been hoping
that they would go check on the warren,
but the rain showed no sign of stopping.

"Oh well. I suppose we're staying
inside today," she sighed. "Maybe I could
read one of Leon's wildlife books. He's

got tons of them in his bedroom."

Arrow sat beside Becky on the window sill as she looked through one of Leon's books. He lifted a fluffy front paw to bat at the raindrops trickling down the pane outside.

Becky laughed. Her friend's cute antics could always cheer her up.

"At least the rabbits will be safe. No one's going to do anything about them in this downpour," she said, giving him a cuddle.

Becky had thought Leon might shut himself away with his computer, but instead he appeared in the sitting room with a big pad of brightly colored paper. "Ever done origami?" he asked.

"Nope," Becky admitted. "But I'll try it!"

Becky soon found out she was pretty good at folding paper into animal shapes. Before long, she was admiring the line of paper animals marching along the coffee table, even though some of them had funny legs.

Leon was really good at origami. He even made an amazing T. rex.

The day passed surprisingly quickly. Delicious smells from the kitchen filled the whole house, making Becky's mouth water. Mrs. Kelly popped her head around the door to say there were cheese crackers and chocolate cake for a snack.

"And I've brought you some of my homemade root beer."

"Wow! What a feast. Can we have it in here on a tray, for a special treat?" Leon asked.

The housekeeper put her hands
on her hips. "What, and get crumbs
everywhere? I don't think so. Come
and sit at the kitchen table."

Becky and Leon exchanged looks,
but did as they were told. As she ate,
Becky crumbled up bits of crackers and
dropped them under the table. Arrow

hopped about eagerly snuffling them all up. She was glad he was invisible or Mrs. Kelly would have had a fit!

"This cake is yummy! Chocolate cream *and* icing with huge chocolate pieces on top!" Leon said. "Killer Kelly might be a pain, but she's an amazing cook!"

After they had finished, Becky, Arrow, and Leon went back to the sitting room.

"What should we do now?" Becky asked, hoping her cousin had some more good ideas.

"I dunno," Leon murmured. His mood seemed to have suddenly changed. "I can't stop thinking about the rabbits, especially Smudge and her kits."

Becky was worried, too, but she always tried to look on the bright side. "You never know. Something might happen to save them."

"Yeah? And pigs might fly!"

Leon looked so troubled that Becky wondered what she could do to cheer him up.

She remembered the stuff she'd read about in the wildlife books. Maybe talking about his favorite subject might take his mind off it—even for just a little while. It was worth a try.

Without really thinking it through, Becky began in a rush. "I never knew that only female rabbits dig burrows. Or that they don't hibernate. And their teeth keep on growing forever . . . ," she said, enthusiastically listing more

facts. She paused for breath and saw Leon glaring at her. "What?"

"The warren's in danger and you don't even care! All you can do is babble on and on, like you're giving a speech or something!"

"I do care!" Becky protested, shocked. "I just thought—"

"Just forget it," Leon muttered. "I wish I'd never taken you to see the warren." He jumped up and left the room.

Becky looked at Arrow in dismay. "Do you think he meant that?" She was ready to go straight after Leon. "I'm going to ask him!"

Arrow laid a tiny soft paw on her arm. "I think Leon needs to be alone."

Becky felt herself calming down as she looked at her wise little friend. Reaching out, she stroked his warm soft ears. "I guess you're right. I guess I was babbling a bit. I just hope that things go back to how they were before. We'd been getting along so well."

Chapter SEVEN

The following day dawned bright and clear. Becky's uncle had planned to drive into the nearest village to take his car to a garage.

Leon followed his dad out into the yard.

Becky hung back a bit. Leon had been quiet at breakfast and they had only exchanged a word or two. She felt awkward with him since their argument.

"Can Becky and I come with you?" she heard Leon ask.

Becky looked up in surprise.

"I could be an hour or two with the mechanic," his dad replied. "Won't you two be bored?"

"Nah. We can go to the library and then I'll show Becky around town." Leon glanced at her over his shoulder and gave an apologetic grin. "Are you coming or what?"

"You bet!" Becky jumped at the chance of an outing, especially since Mrs. Kelly had just declared that she was going to spring-clean the downstairs rooms.

Her uncle smiled. "Come on then, you two."

"Let me run upstairs and grab my bag," Becky said.

Becky found Arrow sitting on her bed, grooming himself. "Yay! Leon's fine with me now and we're all going into the village. Do you want to get into my bag? You'll be safer in there."

Arrow nodded eagerly.

Uncle Den started the car and then pulled out onto the farm road. Becky sat in the back of the car with her bag on the seat beside her, so Arrow could peer out at the countryside.

Sunshine poured down on a patchwork of fields and the green hills in the distance. Becky saw sheep on hillsides and herds of black-and-white cows. Now and then she saw a rabbit feeding on a patch of grass and felt a new pang of concern for the warren above Foxglove Farm.

Uncle Den dropped them at the library, and after spending time looking around at the books, they wandered through the village. Arrow peered out of the bag and his nose twitched at the interesting smells. Becky smiled to

see him enjoying himself. The three
of them passed by a cottage that had a
fancy iron gate topped by a handsome
iron rabbit.

A shaft of sunlight caught the gate
and threw a large dark rabbit-shaped
shadow onto the pavement right in front
of Arrow.

The magic bunny's eyes rolled in
fright. "My enemies have found me!"
Leaping out of the bag, he landed on
the pavement and shot down the street
like a rocket.

"Oh no!" Becky gasped.

Without a second thought, she
hurtled down the street after her tiny
friend, who was already far ahead of her.
Becky just glimpsed his bobtail flashing
as he disappeared around a corner.

"Hey! Where are you going? Wait for me!" Leon cried behind her.

Becky didn't look around. Her heart was in her mouth. She felt frantic at the thought of the dangers of traffic and people who might accidentally trip over her invisible friend.

Rounding the corner, she got a glimpse of the village green ahead. There was an ancient-looking tree in the center. A wooden bench stood beneath it. Becky spotted a familiar little figure cowering underneath it.

"Arrow!" she gasped, weak with relief.

She ran over to him, threw herself onto the grass and reached under the bench. "You're safe now," she crooned. Holding his trembling little body, she

explained about how the shadow rabbit
had appeared.

She could feel Arrow's tiny heart
beating fast as she sank onto the bench
with him and gently stroked his fluffy
pale coffee-colored fur.

"I am sorry, I panicked. Thank you
for coming to find me."

"I'm just glad you're okay," Becky
said fondly. She didn't know what she'd
do if anything happened to her magical
friend.

Leon ran across the green toward Becky and Arrow. "There you are!" he puffed. "Why did you run off like that?"

Becky thought fast. "It was a game of tag. First one to the tree. And I won!" she improvised quickly.

He looked puzzled. "So how come you didn't tell me it was a race?"

Becky shrugged. "It was more fun this way."

"You're weird!" Leon shook his head slowly.

"That makes two of us!" she replied spiritedly.

Leon pretended to look offended. Then he grinned and plonked himself onto the bench beside her. "Fair enough. Maybe that's why we get along."

They both started laughing. Becky was delighted to hear her cousin thought they were getting along, too.

Becky relaxed, enjoying the shade under the old tree. She wondered what Leon would say if he knew that there was an invisible magic bunny so close to him.

She glanced idly toward some shops opposite the green and saw her uncle coming out of one of them. "Look, there's Uncle Den . . ." she began, and then her heart sank as she noticed the sign above the door that read A & R. WILSON. PEST CONTROL SPECIALISTS.

"Oh no!" she groaned. Her uncle had decided to take drastic action to protect his crops.

Chapter EIGHT

That evening, Becky was going downstairs with Arrow when she heard raised voices coming from inside the kitchen.

"So what's wrong with rabbit-proof fences?" Leon demanded.

"I've already told you. They're just not practical on a farm this size," his dad replied patiently. "We use a lot of big machinery and need easy access to the fields. Not to mention the huge cost of new fencing. It's the same with trapping and moving the rabbits. It would just take too long and in the meantime more crops would be lost."

"But what you're planning to do . . . it's horrible!" Leon sounded close to tears.

"I don't like this situation, either. But I have to do what's best for the farm. You're a farmer's son, Leon, and you must learn to be realistic." Becky thought Uncle Den sounded weary, as if he was tired of arguing. "The pest control people will be here tomorrow. They'll do a good job. No rabbits will suffer."

"I won't let you do this!" Leon

yelled. "There's got to be some other way—"

"That's enough!" his dad replied. "I don't want to hear another word."

Leon stormed out of the kitchen and ran upstairs past Becky. She heard the kitchen door slam behind her uncle.

Becky sighed and her shoulders drooped. "Did you hear that? We've only got until tomorrow to think of a way to make Uncle Den change his mind."

Arrow nodded sadly. His dewy brown eyes, with their rainbow twinkles, looked troubled.

They went into the garden so Arrow could eat some grass. As Becky sat watching him, she found herself looking toward the hills beyond the woods.

Something about those steep green slopes got her thinking.

"There must be tons of grass on those hills and they're miles away from anywhere," she said. "Why can't the rabbits go and live there, where no one would bother them?"

Arrow pricked up his ears. "It is a good idea, Becky. But it could take a long time to persuade Smudge and the others to leave their home. They would want to explore the new place first by sending out scouts and then move gradually if all was well."

Becky bit her lip as she thought of the difficulty of persuading hundreds of rabbits to move in just a few short hours. It seemed almost impossible, but she wasn't prepared to give up yet.

The germ of an idea started to form.

"I know magic bunnies can't talk to wild rabbits," she said to Arrow. "But you said you could sense Smudge's thoughts in pictures, didn't you?

Arrow nodded. "That is right."

"So—if you needed to tell her something really important, you could imagine it in pictures and she'd be able to understand you?" Becky asked.

"I do not know. But I could try."

"Okay. This is what I think we

should do." Becky warmed to her idea. "We wait until everyone's asleep tonight, then we go to the warren and . . ."

As she finished explaining, Arrow's whiskers twitched excitedly. "It is a good plan!"

Later that evening, Arrow was curled up on Becky's bed. Outside the window, a glorious sunset had spread flame colors across the darkening sky.

"I'm just going to run downstairs to tell Uncle Den and Leon that I'm having an early night," Becky said. "I don't want anyone coming in later and seeing that I'm not there."

She found Uncle Den and Leon in the sitting room. Leon was sitting hunched in a chair with his arms folded. He looked miserable as he thought about what was to happen the following morning. Becky wished she could tell him what she and Arrow planned to do, but it had to remain a secret.

"Good night, honey. Sleep tight," her uncle said.

Back upstairs, Becky got into bed

with her clothes on and lay there cuddling Arrow. She was sure that she was far too excited to sleep.

But she must have dozed off because it seemed like only moments later when she felt Arrow nudging her cheek urgently with his damp nose.

"Wake up. We must go!"

Chapter
NINE

Bright moonlight flooded the garden. Becky peered out of the kitchen door with Arrow by her feet as she got ready to run toward the gap in the hedge. But then suddenly she felt a familiar warm tingle down her spine as Arrow's key flashed and a big whoosh of crystal dust swirled around her like a small tornado and instantly transported them both to the top of the hill.

"Whoa!" Becky steadied herself after the amazing journey. She loved magic! She checked to see that Arrow was okay, too, and noticed that the little bunny's key was still flashing. Before she could wonder why, Becky felt a light and fizzy whoosh run through her—just like bubbling soda—and she looked down to see her own feet had turned into grayish-brown paws!

Paws? Next to her, Arrow seemed to have grown in size. Oh, wow! She was a wild rabbit!

"Cool!" Becky blinked in amazement. Everything looked extra bright and clear through her large rabbit eyes.

"This way," Arrow told her, hopping toward the warren. "We must find Smudge."

As Becky moved forward, she immediately tripped over in a messy tangle of legs and paws. It wasn't very easy with four feet! Taking a deep breath, she tried again. This time she managed a rather wobbly hop, but the

next one was better and she soon got
the hang of it.

"Wait for me!" she called, chasing
after Arrow.

As they got closer to the warren,
they saw dozens of rabbits hopping
about above ground. Some were
feeding, while others kept watch. Becky
spotted a large gray-brown rabbit with
six kits in tow.

"Smudge!"

Arrow had seen the lead female, too.
He hopped toward her and Smudge
reared up onto her back legs in
welcome.

Becky watched anxiously as Arrow
and Smudge stood with their heads
close together, just as they'd done on
that first visit with Leon. Would Arrow

be able to make Smudge understand that
the whole warren was in great danger
and that they must all move quickly?

Arrow came back toward Becky.

"How did it go?" she asked.

He hunched his furry shoulders. "She
understood, but she is anxious. The
hills seem very far away and she does
not know if the land there is suitable to
make a new warren."

"But it looks perfect!" Becky said.

Arrow nodded. "I think so, too.
That is why I have promised Smudge
that you and I are going to lead them
there."

"We are?" Becky gulped worriedly.
But she trusted her magical friend.
"Um . . . okay then."

She felt the ground vibrate beneath
her paws as first Smudge and then
dozens of other rabbits thumped their
feet. It was the signal for them to leave.
More rabbits poured out of the burrows,
some of them holding kits gently in
their mouths.

And then, headed by Smudge, they
hopped toward Arrow and Becky.

"Ready?" Arrow flashed Becky a
reassuring glance from chocolate-brown

eyes that gleamed with rainbow light.

Becky nodded. As her friend sprang forward, she leaped with him. They kept pace, side by side, as they hopped down the hill and past fields of crops.

Hundreds of rabbits formed a gray-brown stream that seemed to pour after them as they left Foxglove Farm behind. They passed through fields, down paths and across quiet empty roads. When

they reached the woods Arrow sped on, confidently weaving through the trees.

Becky's legs were starting to feel tired by the time they led Smudge and the other rabbits up the slopes of the once-distant hills. At long last Arrow stopped, his sides heaving, and Becky paused beside him.

Smudge hopped over to Arrow. She dipped her head as if to thank him and then snuffled around for a few seconds before scrabbling at the soil with her strong paws. Other rabbits came forward and did the same.

"They're building new burrows!" Becky exclaimed delightedly.

Arrow flicked his tail with great satisfaction. "Yes, Becky. Our work here is done."

Becky felt a warm sense of pride as she looked at all the rabbits working hard to make a new warren. They would be safe here.

But before she could say anything else, she saw Arrow's key flashing again and another cloud of crystal dust surrounded them both.

There was a whooshing sensation and a blur of speed. Becky felt herself landing gently on her behind. She felt soft grass against her hands as she got up. *Hands!* She was a girl again.

She looked around for Arrow and saw him nearby. They were back at the old warren on the hill above Foxglove Farm. It was getting light and the first rays of sunlight gleamed on Arrow's pale fur. Suddenly he leaped into the air,

kicked out his back legs and changed
direction.

"Hey! You did a *binky*!" Becky said.

"Yes. I am happy because we saved
the rabbits!"

"We did, didn't we?" Becky said,
beaming at him. "We're a great team!"

A strange look of happiness mixed
with sadness spread across Arrow's face.

Becky saw that his key was glowing
brightly, as if it had the sun inside it.
The moment she had been dreading
was here. More shimmering crystal dust
appeared, swirling around Arrow and
twinkling with rainbow sparkles.

Suddenly, he appeared in his true
form—a tiny fluffy pale coffee-colored
bunny no longer, but a majestic rabbit
the size of a large cat. His silky pure

white fur was flecked with silver and his large ears had gleaming silver tips.

"Arrow!" Becky gasped. She had almost forgotten how glorious he was. "You . . . you're leaving right now, aren't you?"

He nodded. Rainbows glimmered in his big chocolate-brown eyes. "I must. Moonglow Meadow urgently needs more of the key's magic."

Becky's throat felt tight as she tried to hold back tears. She knew she must be brave and not beg him to stay. "I'll never forget you," she whispered sadly. Rushing forward, she bent down and gathered the handsome white rabbit in her arms.

"You have been a good friend, Becky. I will never forget you either."

Arrow allowed her to give him one final
cuddle and then moved away slowly.
"Farewell, Becky. Remember always to
follow your dreams," he said in a soft
voice.

There was a final flash of light, and
crystal dust showered down around
Becky and tinkled like fairy bells as it

hit the ground. Arrow faded and was gone.

Becky gave in to tears—she knew she was going to miss Arrow a lot.

Something lay on the grass by her feet. It was a single rainbow crystal drop. Wiping her eyes, Becky bent down and picked it up. The drop fizzed against her palm as it turned into a pure white pebble in the shape of a bunny.

Becky slipped it into her pocket. She would keep it as a reminder of the magic bunny and the wonderful adventure they had shared.

"Becky!"

She looked up to see Leon running toward her.

"I came to take one last look at the rabbits, before . . . you know," he said, chewing at his lip. "You weren't in your bedroom, so I guessed you'd be here." He frowned as he saw she was smiling. "What?"

"They're all gone!" she said. "The warren's empty. The rabbits must have left during the night!"

Leon looked puzzled. "I don't get it." He went to investigate and then stood looking at the deserted hillside. "You're right. It even feels different. I don't know what happened, but it's great! I hope Smudge and the others went far away."

"They have," Becky assured him. "I mean . . . I've got a feeling that they've found somewhere even better to live."

"Me too!" Leon beamed at her. "Maybe we could go and look for them? We have got the rest of the week."

"Fine by me!" Becky said happily. She felt proud of what she and Arrow had achieved, even though she could never tell anyone about it.

I hope you get home safely. Take care of Moonglow Meadow, Arrow, she whispered under her breath.

About the AUTHOR

Sue Bentley's books for children often include animals, fairies, and magic. She lives in Northampton, England, in a house surrounded by a hedge so she can pretend she's in the middle of the countryside. She loves reading and going to the movies, and writes while watching the birds on the feeders outside her window and eating chocolate. Sue grew up surrounded by small animals and loved them all—especially her gentle pet rabbits whose fur smelled so sweetly of rain and grass.

Don't miss

Magic Bunny: Chocolate Wishes

Magic Bunny: A Splash of Magic

Don't miss these
Magic Puppy books!

Don't miss these
Magic Kitten books!

Magic Ponies

Don't miss these
Magic Ponies books!